AVA
and the
SKIMPY PICNIC

By Elias Carr

Illustrated by Michael Garton

Book design: Tim Palin Creative

Library of Congress Cataloging-in-Publication Data

Names: Carr, Elias, author. | Garton, Michael, illustrator.
Title: Ava and the skimpy picnic / by Elias Carr ; illustrated by Michael Garton.
Description: Minneapolis : Sparkhouse Family, [2016]. | Summary: Ava the lamb, Rufus the dog, and Jo the goat decide to have a picnic but become greedy and decide to bring only a little bit of what they have gathered.
Identifiers: LCCN 2015046610 | ISBN 9781506410517 (hardcover : alk. paper)
Subjects: | CYAC: Picnics--Fiction. | Greed--Fiction. | Sheep--Fiction. | Dogs--Fiction. | Goats--Fiction. | Christian life--Fiction.
Classification: LCC PZ7.C229323 Av 2016 | DDC [E]--dc23 LC record available at http://lccn.loc.gov/2015046610

The paper used in this publication meets the minimum requirements of the American National Standard for Information Sciences—Permanence of Paper for Printed Library Materials, ANSI Z329.48-1984.

Printed in the United States of America

24 23 22 21 20 19 18 17   2 3 4 5 6 7 8 9 10

VN0004589; 9781506410517; JAN2017

SPARK
HOUSE
FAMILY
sparkhouse.org

One beautiful day, Ava invited Rufus and Jo to a picnic on the big rock. "Let's each bring something to share!" Ava said.

"I'll bring berries!" said Ava.

"I know where to find honey," said Rufus.

"And I can get lots of water," said Jo.
"We must have something to drink."

Ava walked to the berry
bushes. She picked as many
as she could to fill her basket.

Rufus found a tree with a beehive. He lulled the bees to sleep with his horn. Then he pulled out three chunks of honeycomb.

Jo carried three water jars to the stream. He bent down to fill the jars with cold, clear water.

On her way to the picnic, Ava stopped to rest.
She looked at the basket full of berries.

These berries look delicious, she thought. *If I share this basketful, Jo will probably eat most of them. Then I won't have any left. Maybe . . . I'll bring just a few and keep the rest.*

Rufus had to hide from the buzzing bees.

Getting the honey was hard work, he thought. And Ava will probably want all the honeycombs for herself. She loves honey. Maybe . . . I'll bring one piece and keep the others here instead.

Jo lifted the heavy jars and headed to the big rock.

These water jars are so heavy, he thought. *Once we start the picnic, Rufus will probably drink them all! He is always so thirsty. Maybe . . . I'll keep these two near this bush and just bring the smallest jar.*

The friends began walking more quickly to the big rock for their picnic.

I hope Rufus brings lots of honey, thought Ava.

Jo knows how I like to drink lots of water, thought Rufus.

Berries! My favorite! thought Jo. *I bet Ava picked bunches!*

When they arrived at the big rock,
everyone was hungry and thirsty.
"Time for our picnic!" said Ava.

Ava spread her berries on the big gray rock. *Maybe they won't notice I only brought five berries each.*

Rufus put the honeycomb on a smooth, green leaf. *Maybe this leaf will make the honeycomb look bigger.*

Jo sloshed the water around in the cool stone jar. *Maybe they'll think this jar is full of water.*

The friends looked at the berries and the honey and the water. They looked around at one another. Each one knew the picnic wasn't really a picnic. There was barely enough for each of them!

"I was going to share!" each friend said.
"But then . . ."

"I wanted more for myself," said Ava.

"I thought you'd eat it all," Rufus said.

"I didn't want to give you too much," Jo mumbled.

Ava looked around. Rufus was staring at the ground. Jo was looking at the water jar. "I think we need a little help with sharing our food with one another," she said.

Dear God,

Sometimes I want to keep everything to myself.
Next time I have a chance,
help me share with my friends.

Amen.

Then, all at once, each of them knew exactly what to do!

Ava, Rufus, and Jo each ran to get something to share. Then they hurried back toward the big rock.

"I have a whole basket of berries!"

"Here is a honeycomb for each of us!"

"And I brought two more jars
so we would not be thirsty!"

The friends shared all their food
and there was plenty to eat and
drink. Now this was a great picnic!

ABOUT THE STORY

Watch what happens as the friends' picnic ingredients fall short of a feast. A prayer about sharing helps save the day!

DELIGHT IN READING TOGETHER

When you read this story, your voice and facial expressions can show the increased disappointment in the friends as they realize their picnic is not very satisfying.

ABOUT YOUNG CHILDREN AND SHARING

"Mine!" may be one of the first words a child learns to say. It certainly can be one of the loudest! Children need to see sharing modeled many times in many settings by many people. But when you witness their first acts of sharing with others, you'll celebrate this marvelous show of early empathy!

A FAITH TOUCH

God created us to be in community with others. That means sharing when we may want to keep things to ourselves. Learning to give is a lifetime journey. It can begin early with young children seeing how we model generosity in response to God's generous love for us.

Do not neglect to do good and to share what you have, for such sacrifices are pleasing to God.
>   *Hebrews 13:16*

SAY A PRAYER

Share this prayer Ava said when she did not share:

Dear God, sometimes I want to keep everything to myself. Next time I have a chance, help me share with my friends.

Amen.